To my mom and dad
—J.R.

Text copyright © 2005 by Harriet Ziefert Inc.
Pictures copyright © 2005 by Teetersaw, Inc.
All rights reserved
CIP Data is available.
Published in the United States 2005 by
Blue Apple Books
515 Valley Street, Maplewood, N.J. 07040
www.blueapplebooks.com
Distributed in the U.S. by Chronicle Books

First Edition
Printed in China
ISBN: 1-59354-092-2
1 3 5 7 9 10 8 6 4 2

Misery Is a Smell In Your Backpack

drawings by
Jennifer Rapp

Blue Apple Books

Most days you feel spiffy.
Life can't get you down!
The world is your oyster,
Your kingdom, your crown.

But some days you lose it—
You're sulky, you pout.
You can't even think
How to work it all out.

You're stuck in a rut,
Downhearted and blue,
You throw up your hands...
You don't know
    what to do!

Instead of singing
A misery song,
Read on to find out
What else can go wrong!

Misery is when you're warm
in your bed and the floor is cold
and the alarm clock shouts:

"IT'S TIME FOR SCHOOL!"

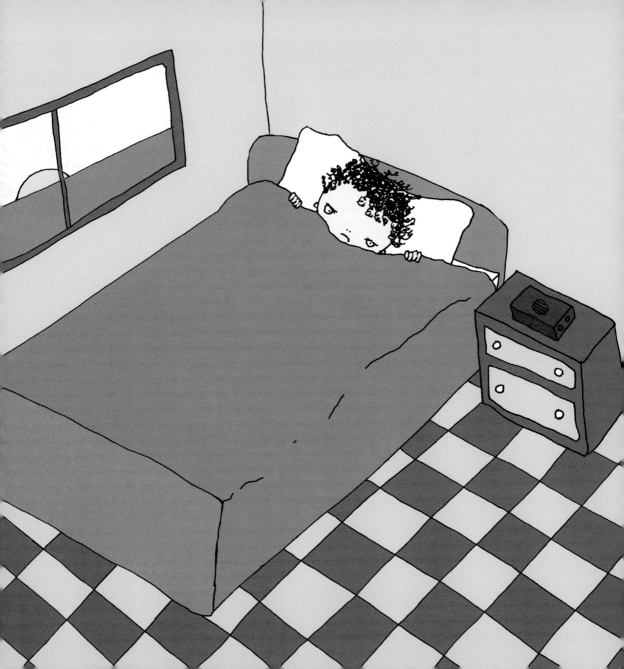

Misery is when your mom
insists on sensible school shoes
and you really want flip-flops.

Misery is rushing from the house
to catch the school bus,
then realizing that you didn't
bring your lunch.

Misery is when
you feel horrible,
rotten, nasty,
dreadful, and mean
and someone says:

Misery is two
against one—
especially if you're not
part of the twosome.

Misery is being in the
way of flying spit
from Susie MacDougal,
who never stops talking.

Misery is learning that you and everyone in your class will be checked for head lice!

Misery is waiting for the nurse to bring you an ice pack and a towel.

Misery is a
friend with
bad breath.

Misery is listening
to your parents
list the 29 reasons
why you can't go
to the mall.

Misery is when
no one but your dog
wants to hang out
with you.

Misery is when
your little sister
asks you and
your boyfriend
where babies
come from.

Misery is getting the dead fish out of the tank.

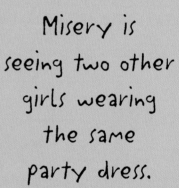

Misery is seeing two other girls wearing the same party dress.

Misery is getting caught
"Instant Messaging"
after you said
you'd be in bed by nine
and asleep by ten.

Misery is when you really
just want to go to sleep
and you find
crumbs in your bed.

Misery is dreaming that the smell in your backpack is a dead mouse.

Some days have miseries
In all kinds of ways.
Hope your tomorrow's
Not one of these days.

Hope in the morning
Not a thing will go wrong.
And you won't be singing
A misery song.